Coope Spur Ski Area

2019

It's a Day for Ski and Play

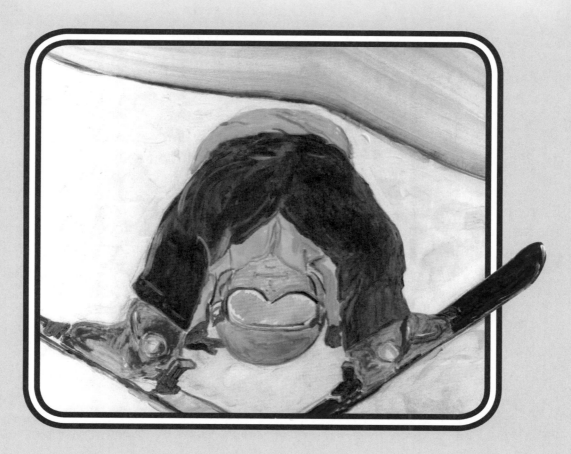

Terri Woods
Illustrated by Tracy Valentine

For The Boys ...

Hooray, hooray, new snow fell last night
The sky is now blue; the sun is out bright
I run to their room. "Wake up," I say
"It's a Bluebird Powder Day!"

Helmets, goggles for the snow
Excitement builds as piles grow
Mittens, fuzzies, coats, and socks
Finding them in our toy box

I have red skis; brother has blue
Hard to focus; must pursue
Gobble down breakfast, load up the car
"Buckle in everyone; the mountain's not far!"

Our smiles are wide as we reach the top
Ready to play at our favorite spot
The grown-ups will take turns
to ski the deep snow
While we look for the powder
in the playground below

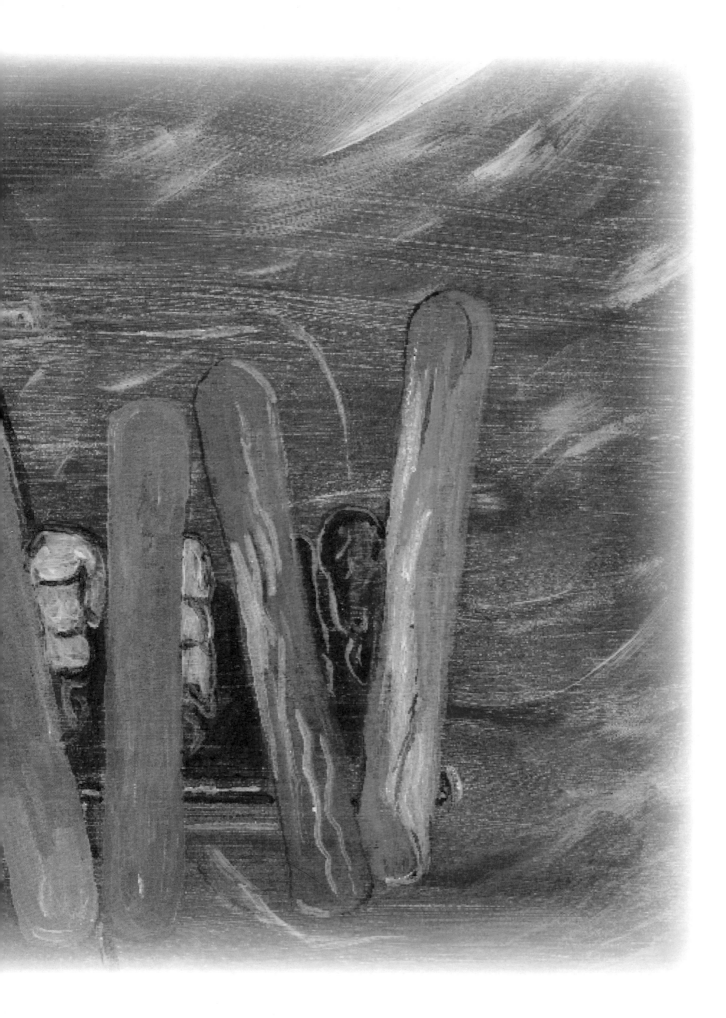

Rock-paper-scissors,
Mommy wins first rights
Shovel-probe-transceiver,
and a partner for her hike
Daddy, me and Brother,
up the chair we go
We all can't wait to play
in the new-fallen snow

Diamonds sparkle in the light
Laying fresh tracks is pure delight
Flying free on freshly groomed
All the magic ; All consumed

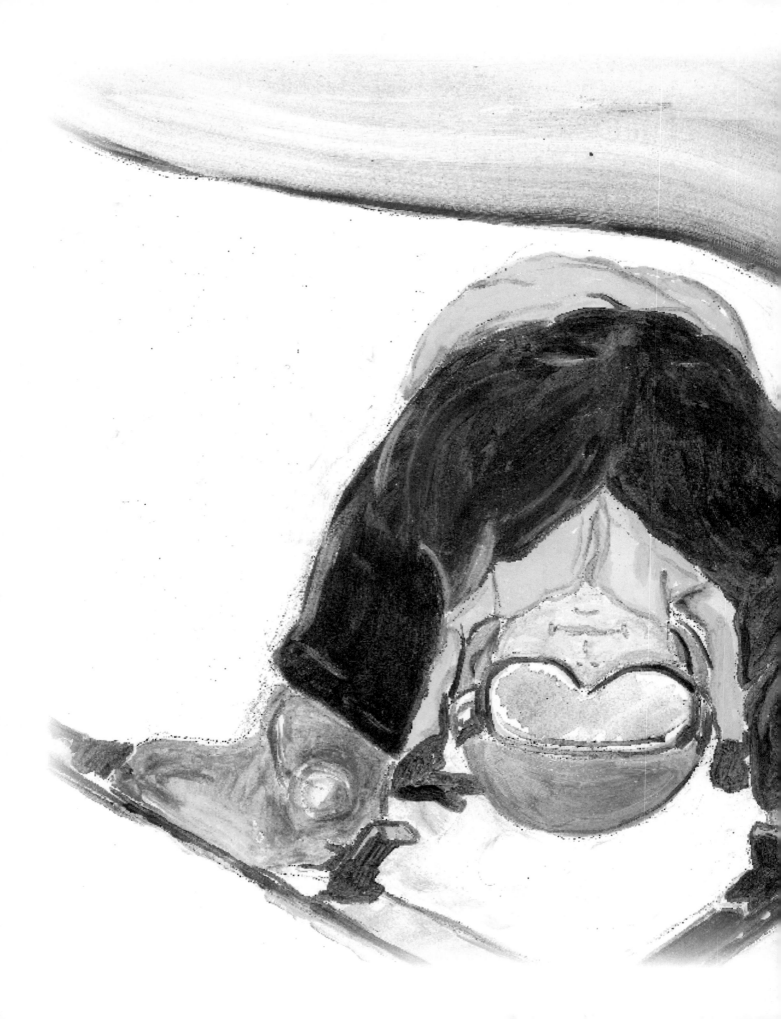

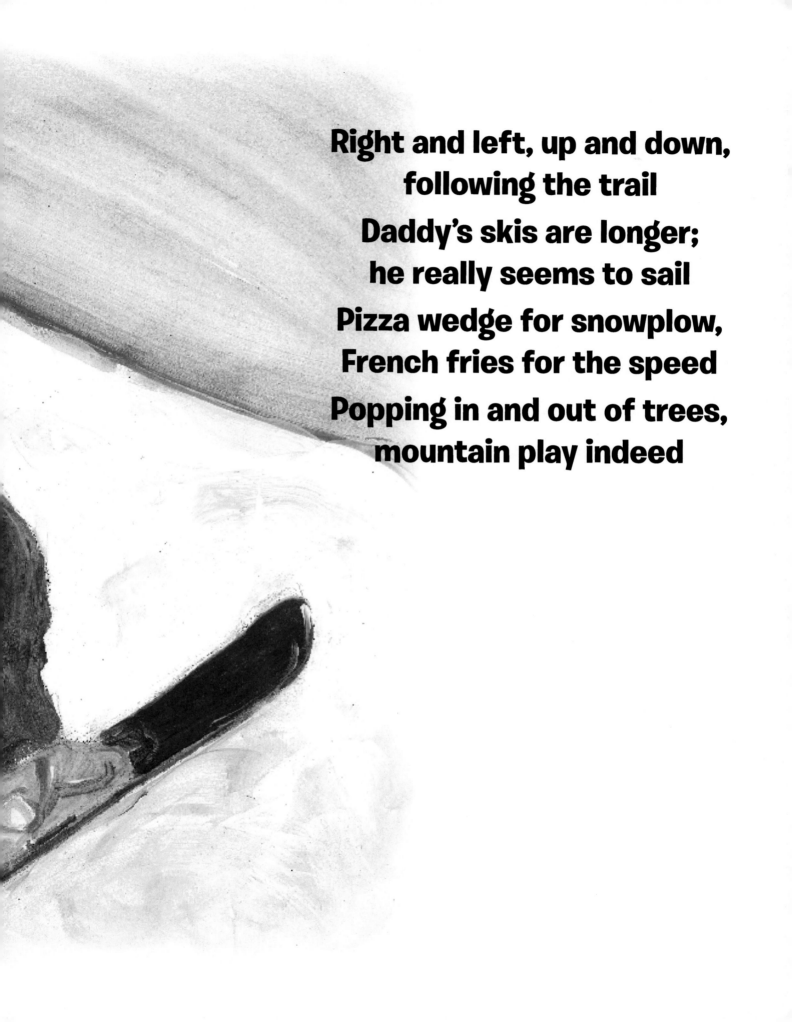

Right and left, up and down,
following the trail

Daddy's skis are longer;
he really seems to sail

Pizza wedge for snowplow,
French fries for the speed

Popping in and out of trees,
mountain play indeed

Daddy's turn to hike the ridge,
searching for the fluff

Look up high to see his line;
he'll join us soon enough

In the lodge, by the fire,
make a little nest

We need to fill our bellies
and take a little rest

Mountain's getting busy; time to hide away
Skiing all the pockets we find late in the day
It's fun to hit some kickers, pop a little air
Brother is my spotter; Mommy says a prayer

One more time up the chair,
heading for the sun

Family time together,
it really is such fun

Daddy's skiing backward;
Mommy tries ballet

Figure eights down the slope,
we all are young at play

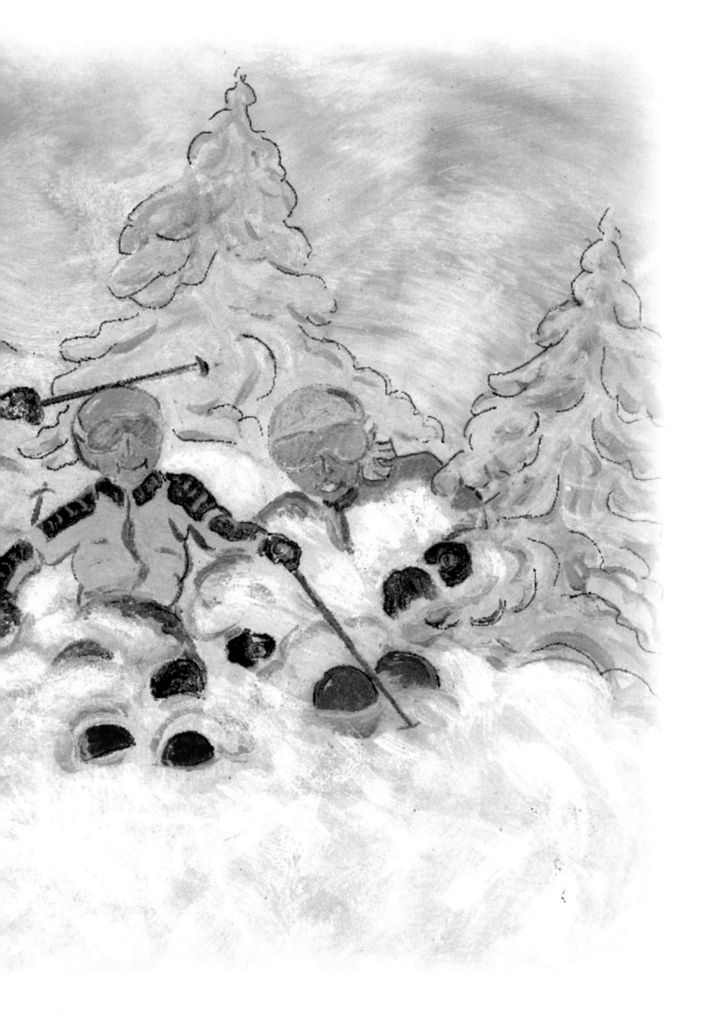

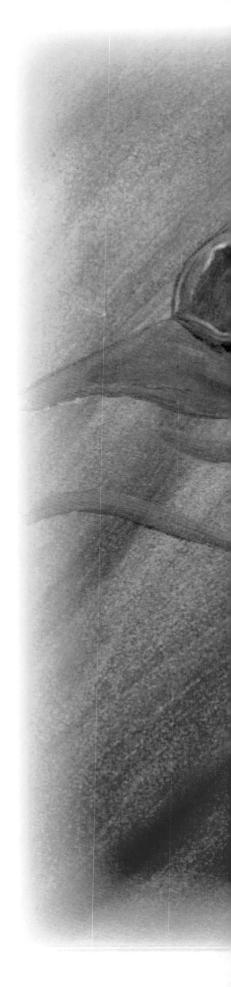

Hooray, hooray, we got to play;
we got to play all day

We say good-bye, just for now;
it's hard to drive away

Back at home already,
we're tucked into our beds

Wishing, watching, waiting
for the next new storm to shred

Author - Terri Woods

Terri lives in the heart of the Cascade Mountains with her favorite ski partners, her husband and her two boys. Skiing has been a joy from the first ski school bus trip up to Stevens Pass as a 5th grader, to working at the ski area for years, to sharing with her own boys the joy of the mountains. The ski community has provided her with years and years of laughter, smiles, and profound comfort when needed. This book was written for all the future little skiers out there and their families to remember, never stop playing....."

Illustrator - Tracy Valentine

Tracy, a lifelong skier, met and befriended the author, while ski patrolling at Stevens Pass Ski Area, Washington State. With her lifetime of ski experiences, and her background in art and graphic design, she was able to paint the pictures the author envisioned as she was writing this story.

Made in the USA
San Bernardino, CA
31 January 2019